SCHOLASTIC

Let's Find Out

My REBUS Reader

Spring Is Just Bee-ginning!

by Pamela Chanko

SCHOLASTIC INC.

New York Toronto London Auckland Sydney New Delhi Hong Kong

What did the  see? It saw spring .

bee

flowers

What did the  see? It saw spring .

bee rain

What did the  see? It saw spring .

bee vegetables

What did the  see? It saw a spring .

bee

bunny

What did the  bee see? It saw a spring  bird.

What did the  see? It saw a spring .

bee

frog

What did the  bee see? It saw more  bees!